The Evil of Business

- - - - - - - - - - - - - - - -

The Hidden Principles of Business

Brendon Mokalapa

Special Gratitude ...

The Almighty have Blessed this writing so humongous, hence first Special Thanks are directed to HIM. Further special gratitude goes to the reader of this book, fellow colleagues in the faculty of philosophy, writing and Education for the undoubted inspiration and motivations.

Extended thanks to the featured names in this book, as the agreed to be used as non-fictional instances to deepen the view of the book.

Content...

Hidden Principles of Business

Chapter One

Desires of Business

It is so motivating to see one successful businessman or businesswoman, to hear of what they have and how much they own. It is so good, that almost everyone who observes would wish and love to have such possessions in life. Who does not want to be like the South African Motsepe? Or like the Chinese Jack Ma? Like the Norwayan Yngve Slyngstad, Polandian Zygmunt Solors-Zak, or Argentinian Eduardo Eurnekian?

Some of who you have not even heard of, yes, they are successful in business, that once you just hear a little bit about them, you would love to be like them, or just meet them and have a little talk with them and where they advise you. Or even worse, to just see them. You would be motivated to grow in business. Well, this following writing is to show you a secret side or business which is wide clear to some and one which widens the opportunity of business when having observed.

I believe that all these businessmen and women like Chimamanda Ngozi Adiche have such a character I will share as we go on with the in this book and they have it in their natural genes.

One thing about business that you must notice is that business has no gender, but it depends on the mentality. Many failing businesses have people who think they are already successful when they just conclude one chapter and enter another. Business does not care about gender; it is us as stereotypic people who view certain businesses being good for certain genders. But business has no eyes that see the private part, or the type of hormone present in one's body. Rather, business can read the head, the mind and how bad you want it. Not the mere desire for it without action and not the lust of it without an inch of motion.

It would be evil to count all businesswomen and forget Netherlander, Charlene de Carvalho-Heineken, a single mother of five that managed to work hard to keep the fire burning. This is just to show you that sometimes you do not begin a business from scratch, but you must keep it moving. And most people make a big mistake by thinking that starting a business from scratch and keeping a business moving are two far different things. No, they are not. Because the only difference will be the genesis of both sides, but they will go under same challenges.

Both businesses (One which was started from scratch and one which was found already running) will have to work hard to keep up with times. Not like some companies did, which a father started it, grew it, left it to the children, and the children ran it the same way their father did in a different time interval. That made many businessmen and businesswomen turns into nothing but being regular society members who have only memories. Yet, with this mother of five, Heineken, she found a running business and continued to have shares in it, and side hustles. She maintained such status of being in business until her death.

To just lay the matter on the table, many people, almost everyone has a desire of business, whether to start it or to continue it. But one thing they do not know is that starting it is not hard, finding a business that you can continue is not hard, though it might take time, but to keep the business running is a hell of a game.

Business is not starting some small thing, famous thing, and nice thing you call business, but business is about keeping the fires burning. Businessmen are not people who started something, but people who began and continued to keep the fires burning, where the beginning is quite easy and the actual action of keeping it running is the rot to bear.

Do you think it was hard for Mark to think of a social media? App like Facebook? Or was it easy to do the actual App and keep it running? Remember, when you start, the only trouble is the resources and the spirit to begin, but once started, you start to have haters, testers, deriders, sometimes financial sacrifices to keep the business running and bad workers. When you start, everyone around seems to have the zeal for work, like when you hire someone, they show and pretend to have all that you need, but as time goes by, there need to be some cut of stuff. When Mark thought of Facebook, there was not much friction, but once he started it, hackers appeared from nowhere and criticizers started flooding.

Should you go to the street and ask any random people about their idea for business, many will tell you if not all, a certain nice and even mountain shaking plan for business, that the only thing needed is resource. Well, that way, business has started, it is conceived, they need to nurture it, make the belly grow until it is born, then they keep it alive. That is, it. Any business idea is like a sperm cell to your head, and then you need to like it, love it, use whatever that is around to keep it developing in that head, and then keep it growing with anything that will work positively toward it until it can be born.

By being born, I mean that it must be implemented and known. And once it is known, it is born. So, it needs soft food first to grow, and solid food when grown. Until it can survive on its own without you. Patience is needed there. But the starting of business is when you think it. Elon Musk started Space-X the minute he thought of it and gave birth to it by just doing what you read here.

When a baby is born, the mother does not delay the development of the baby because there are certain things which are not there, rather she uses anything around that can be good for developing the baby. Develop that business. Use anything around you. Even if it means sacrificing, if you love that child of yours, you will do anything for them, just to keep them up.

It is the desire of a business that makes people hate successful businesspeople, because they want to be in their positions, but cannot, because they lack the inside push for business. That is also jealous. Business does not need desire, because once you fulfil the desire, you relax, and that is eviler than the evil of business. The reason many have ideas of business but no business to show you, is because they have plenty of desire for it, but nothing to push them to it.

They have resources and still look for more, you give them that more, and they look for infinite more. The more people you ask about their business ideas on how they started, you will notice that for more than half the people, the idea started because of longing someone's business, or having developed the desire to surpass someone's business. Genuine business ideas are those which just began from almost nothing.

Like when I developed the little desire for a business too, I started off with fireworks, since I saw the landlord selling them. I sold them for her as she requested, and when she dropped her business, I made it my own. Notice that I did not start it, but found it running, but that was not the problem. The problem was to keep it running. I had so much little in me to push the business. But the fact that I had something in me, it really did help in making that business run for more than three years. I made a lot of money for a child that I was at the age of 16 to 20, getting about maximum of R400 profit in a day.

That was a lot of money. Some people around me also developed desires for such a business, and even decreased prices to attract all customers. I had that little thing in me, the intrinsic aid, which was the love for business, so, that competition did not shake me. They came and fell, and finally

I would still be the one standing. That proved to me, that they had desire and lust but no push from within.

I proceeded by small business, but as time went by, challenges were many. Some documents like license were needed. So, because I had a little thing to push me moving, I did not push harder. I got scared and dropped the business. I did not drop it because of small challenges, but because of big challenges. So, I noticed that if I had a big love for such a business, I was going to get the license and continue selling. Maybe now many would know me as a big fire work seller. The baby is less challenged when still new-born, for the first few months or years, then as it is growing and getting tougher; it will be more and more challenged. Same applies in business. The baby has less stress when it's young, and the stress increases with time and maturity. Some businesses noticed this and refused to grow.

Whatever you think, is because of something that happened. You cannot just think of a business, either you were motivated by someone, or desired something you saw or heard of, and then started thinking. And the more time you invest on thinking, you end up coming up with something which was never seen, might be a familiar genre, but new style. It will not need desire to make that thing develop and grow, no, because already it might have used desire to be conceived. So, you need love, deep love for that idea, and you will give it all you have to ensure it lives, even if it means you are dying but it is remaining.

You give that little baby of yours a mother's love, that you can get into a burning flat just to rescue it. Well, many might argue, but that is the level of love I am speaking of. When I say you must have that thing in you, it is love. But sadly, some might not know the difference between love and desire. Well, love is from within, it is within, and only goes out to show itself. But a desire is from outside, goes in and comes out to show itself. How you notice is by seeing the challenges that shake you, if they finish you, and you do not wake up, then it was all desire. If you are shaken and you stand, fall and stand, countless times, then it is love. If you can go and research about how many times the South African born Elon Musk failed in his ideas, but there he is, still standing. That is love, not a desire.

So, do have love for the ideas you have, and know that love is not self-made, it is created by your personality sometimes, and other elements, but it is grown by you about how you think and how much you research. For an instance, when you love a person, you didn't create that love yourself, no, but you had that strong thing from the inside which made you fall for the person. But just standing there amazed will not make you love the person a lot, what will make you love them more is when you start researching about them, finding things which incline with your personality, then you start loving them more and the love grows.

Imagine loving a lady, and find out that she is a party animal, while you are a raw believer, that will decrease the love a bit. And as for a desire, it is self-made, it is caused by things like jealous and lust, lack of self-control, lack of gratitude and felicitations. You then develop and desire and grow it more when you hear more of the person and how good they describe them. The desire is always for a short-while, I mean, once you get what you wanted, you satisfy the desire and leave it. Hence these days we see a girl having been into many relationships at the age of 15. It is all desires, and not love. So, even for business, have love, not desire.

And that love, you might have love for a certain kind of business, and not another. So, follow the kind of business you have love for. One you notice you do not have love, leave it, don't bother, because sooner or later you will give up as challenges flood in.

Chapter Two

Undermining Small Businesses

Having a strong desire for business is as much as having big, powdered muscles, sooner or later they run out. Better follow what you love, not what you desire. And another problem of many businesspeople is the desire for big businesses, while undermining small businesses. That is toxic to many ideas, because a child does not just start by being an adult when conceived, they rather are conceived, developed, born, developed further, grown with sacrifices, surpassing challenges, and passing trials and hate, then grow big to be independent.

So, people want the final product after just getting the first reactant. And their fall in business is great. People who want to succeed in business in just few months and years and simply small eagles which want to fly out of the nest when not knowing how to walk first. Their fall from the nest to the ground is great, and thus ends up dying out of ideas when down there.

Every business, whether you start it afresh or found it moving, it is always starting from childhood stage, which is where it is regarded as small business, not known by many, but known.

Such small businesses can remain small or grow into independence. You know of adults who are still children, who still live under their parent's roofs. Years have gone by, that they were even supposed to be out there independent, but sadly, they did not develop the wings to fly out, so, they remained children. There are businesses which are forever small.

What is a small business? Well, I would say, it is any implemented idea which will fall the minute the owner is not present. In legal arena, a business is regarded a person, hence, I like giving an instance of it as a baby, so you can gurgitate it better and assimilate it to your brain. Having an idea for business, sometimes you have this big idea, so big and forget that it all starts small, hence end up not having that idea done. Sometimes you have a small idea and implement it, but forget to grow that small idea, hence, end up remaining small. But at least you have started.

Let me show you how ignorant many people are toward small businesses. With the definition of ignorance as having the dangerous ability to see, but still think it is not real. I will give you the short synopsis of my mom's business, though it is still small, but I will share it. When I grew up, the few scenic memories I still have remained in my brain. I remember my mom used to sell tomatoes, fruits, and vegetables, having a small market at the street. I only recall one case, but as she narrates, I can see it is not just a thought, but a memory. But her business died on the road as I grew up and she found a job and so much happened. I believe she had not much to push her from within, so, she was challenged and succumbed to small challenges. She had a small business since it died and decomposed the minute she was no longer there.

Nevertheless, I saw that she had love for business. So, after having years of no business, but piece-jobs, some good and some bad, she noticed that she doesn't last in the work field and needed to go back to her business world.

She recently started by selling ice-pops. She had an idea, and then developed it, sacrificed some little money, and now she is having that small business because if she leaves it with the family, it goes down. She even needed to buy an extra fridge to allow it grow. But sadly, she was not ready to sacrifice that much, though her reasons for not buying it were understandable. But in business, we do not listen to the negativity.

And notice that negativity is not the same as critique. Negativity is anything that will pull the business down, yet a critique is anything that will help the business grow wisely and strong, things like speaking of future obstacles and humps, not speaking of things you cannot do at all, no, but things you cannot do which might harm the business if you do it.

That is the evil of business, because it is selfish, and it needs you to think of itself alone. That you can even sacrifice everything around you just to give that business. She can sell the fridge she has, and buy a bigger one, that is courage. It is what can make her become big in business, so, the fact that she is not willing to go that big, and then it shows she has so little love for business. She does not think on the growth of the business by any means, but still thinks about the surrounding.

She can sell the television to get both money and space, and buy a bar fridge, then make more cash later, and buy a new television set, as for space, she can think of it. The evil of business is that it has no pity for humanity; it is evil in that way because it can do whatever at its stake to grow, even if it means getting many unemployed and killed. That is purely evil. We can employ the Philosophy of many like Isaiah Berlin, Immanuel Kant and so forth, they will communicate with you through writing, that indeed it is evil thing that is done by business. But what can we say, we love business, and we sometimes need it?

Anyway, I have just shared with you a bit about my mom, on how much potential she has in being effective like Wangari Wa-Muthai, also known as Wangari Maathai, she started small, in the business of planting trees. She started so small with less challenges. When she continued planting trees by passion and love, she ended up planting as much trees as she could possibly do, that when big challenges came, like a whole country state going against her tree planting, she continues. When she survived assassinations because of the trial to stop her from planting trees, she continued planting more trees.

She did not stop, pushed from the inside, not by desire, but love and by passion. She loved planting trees, though for various reasons, but let us focus on her success of planting 3 million trees in 30 years. That's a huge success. Some would have planted only a thousand and feel like they done enough, no, enough is done when what you have done can still survive into generations. As we speak, there is a forest named after her, which is now a tourist site, and all trees in that forest were planted by her. She became little bit known, then more known, and now she is so much known. That is how businesses exist and grow. But many ignore the small businesses.

They undermine small businesses, thinking they are of no help to their very big ideas. That is the biggest mistake a big thinking person can ever make. Do not undermine the small thinkers. Remember Albert Einstein? He was thought of being a small thinker at school, when he did his own things during laboratory practical, and even kicked out of school, but few years down the line, he was employed to come back to the same school to teach them his methods. Imagine. Being undermined for being small, and later, you sponsor them.

Never undermine a small thing, because even a mustard grain is the smallest when starting, but big inside when it is revealed, and grow more to make a forest. Start small while thinking big. Ensure your small thing will get big and have a big heart for big ideas. Also have big love for big plans. Do small, while having huge in you. It is the principle of business. Ask many and read their books.

By looking a bit back at the life of a South African boxer, Jacob "Baby-Jake" Matlala. He was regarded and seen as the shortest heavyweight Boxer of the world. When he was going to fight, his opponents would undermine him a lot and looking at him as a small person to be effective. But they did not know what was inside. They simply looked at him and concluded without going into the depth and the heart of the man. It is like that in business. Many businesses seem to be too small to the look, so small to be making millions, but they are even sponsoring big organizations. They are small by look, but effective by act. This has been a lesson to me from long, that I should not judge the income of a company by its status. Many famous businesses are bankrupt, while non-famous businesses are making millions. That is the effectiveness of a small business.

It is true that many small businesses remain small, but not all of them. And even those which remain small, just try to find out more about them and you will notice something you did not know about them. Can you remember an existing small business which was there when you grew up? And the business seems to be not growing? Such a business is small, but effective. That might have been the goal of the owner when they started it. Back then, that goal was a hit, but since times change, now that goal seems small. Do not undermine it at all.

Let me share with you about one of my brothers by common faith, not biological, but a businessman by title. He is having a very small business to many, but to me, I already see it being big after having observed his heart, his passion, and his desire for business. He is not stopped by mere challenges. He overcomes challenges which would cease many dreams of business, but he is still maneuvering. It would be a mistake for me to start such a lovely topic with you and not talk about a hard-working, passionate businessman like Michael Nkosana Mbhalathi.

I went to the same school with him and was in the same accounting class with his sister. That is where I can recklessly say the business thing is running in his family's blood, but maybe I can be right since even his mother is actually a businesswoman. They are both working on the same business, Michael, and his mom. It is an overwhelming thing to have noticed and experienced the daily activity of his business. It is too small to many as I mentioned that they even think it makes only bread money, but, out of their ignorance, they do not know that he is even able to buy the most expensive phone with a month's profit. Think about that.

The brother is running a small business where he is selling cakes and little other stuff to school learners during lunch. I joined him the other day and experienced how tiring the business was. I could not sleep later that day due to having been exhausted. He was selling at about four different schools, having two people to help him, and his mother at the other side. He would leave to school with a wheelbarrow or having requested an Uber and return walking empty handed. I thought he was making cents, but I noticed that from the single school, he was making a profit of about R400 in a day. With about R1600+ profit, not counting the costs that returned, but only the money that the business generated. That shocked me, to notice that in a month he can generate more than R5000 from that business.

Then I wondered why people undermine small businesses like that. Is it because they are not registered? Or because they do not have names? Or do not formally have a place to work at? And what does a name matter in business? Is it not the fact of making it represent itself? I stopped undermining small businesses that day. It was tiring but gaining more profit beyond thought. And the cakes were sold at a very low price to be thought of making such money.

I then noticed why the ladies who sold at school during my schooling time really sold for a living. They made more money than teachers, yet teachers were respected more than those ladies. With teachers working all day, and those ladies only for an hour, but the opposite of gain happened.

Business can make millions, no matter how small or big it is. Just proper planning, dedication and not leaving the love for it out. Love it with your heart, and you will not even feel the anxiety it gives you; you will only feel the profit it floods your way daily. I have also thought deep and questioned myself about the women who sat all day at a vegetable and fruits market. With me witnessing very few customers buying. I thought about their costs, at how much they use for transport to go and buy the products, the costs of materials used, and they sell the products at a lower price, yet at the end of the year they manage to go to their countries and spend the whole December holidays there.

I even thought maybe they have other businesses on the other side, but after noticing Michael, I then knew they made enough money for all those activities. I thought of only what I saw, which is how they really cope with the rotting products but did not have full information about their businesses. I undermined them through ignorance to the business view side of their work.

I lost the appetite of undermining small businesses the minute I revealed the truth behind their capabilities. I even hungered to have a small business too, but not limit it to being small, but nurture it to grow as much as it can, and I am on my way to do so. I will cease every opportunity to do business but will be limited by the wickedness that will have to be done to ensure business stands. I will not betray humanity that much just for the sake of business being healthy. No, I cannot. I would take opportunities such as being involved in infant businesses that arise around me. I would put a hand in every business that needs a hand and put a leg to any that needs a leg. If I would be part of the body organs of that business. Even if it means I get the lowest position, if I am in and witnessing its growth, then look for me in it, and you will find me.

If a baobab tree never starts small, then I would never wish to start from those small businesses. The thing is, I never know which one will boom and which one will succeed. So, like in gambling, I bet all numbers and expect the results eagerly so. This is not gambling, though I liken to it, because here, I can bet all numbers without obviously loosing, but with the probability to gain more than I lost. In gambling, the system is wise that if you bet all numbers, you would use more money than you will gain, it is a must. Though gambling on its own is a business.

I have ceased looking at small businesses as everyone else look at them, not because I do not look at the structure that is seen, but at the skeletons and at how it manages to remain standing. I stopped undermining small businesses, so also stop that, and you will see a wider range of chance to succeed.

Chapter Three

Business And Religion

Just a further look at the fact that business is quite evil, many questions might rise about business and religion. When coming to this, I recall the words of the mighty Al-Ghaddafi when he said, "A political leader that is religious is leading people to hell." That is quite true, since it is vividly seen that politics and religion do not mix. They are water and oil. That does not mean they do not come to touch, but they do not mix.

They can be in one place, but not agree. Look at the rules of all political parties in power, somewhere somehow, they defy Scripture. Yes, a small political party might have rules which go inclined with Scripture fully, but as they go up the slope towards leading the country, even the rules increase distance from the Scriptures. Yes, the Scriptures of any religion. Because religion is not a national thing, and as for politics, they are national. To get as many people as possible, get to be wide in your considerations.

Donald Trump confessed it well when he said what the Americans wanted to hear when he wanted to be in power. Is it that not true to him? And is that not lies or hypocrisy? And is that not against religion?

Same measure goes to business and religion, but just a little different. There is evil in business. You will see more reasons for this thesis by the time your current reading cease. There is evil in business, while religion does not entertain evil, unless it is evil religion. To say business and religion do not mix, does not mean they cannot meet. As I write, I do have a business too, which is having some religion inside. I will narrate it to you soon, as for now, let me share with you how business and religion meet and not mix.

What do I mean when I say they can meet but not mix? Well, look at oil and water. Don't they meet? Can't you put them both in one cup? And shake? You can. So, if you can ever mix at the end of the mixing, you will have one pure substance? No, that is what I mean. They can meet but cannot mix. Like politics and religion. There are religious political parties out there, but they never mix. There are religious businesses, but they never mix. I have one.

It is either they will be more skewed for the politics or more to the religion. There is this religious political party I know, you might know, a South African one. It has existed back then, even before I was born. It is supported mainly by one tribe, Zulus. Inkatha Freedom Party (IFP). Which was founded in 1975. It has been almost stationary for over three decades. It is because it tried to merge politics, tribe, and religion. But it does not grow, and even so, it is still skewed to one side, the political side. Since it is more famous in politics than in religion and tribe. Should I mention the Zulu tribe, it might take you hours to think of IFP. If I think of religion, it might take you days to think of IFP, but the minute I mention South African politics, you will take seconds before you can mention this party.

Just to elucidate to you more on business and religion, let me touch the garment of my own developing biography, and tell you about my clothing business. It was in the stomach of the year 2019 when I felt maximum academic pressure. Especially from Chemistry. I had so many thoughts of dropping out, or even dropping school and going to work, because it was not working out well. Fortunately, I had legends around me, who already stepped where I was stepping and showed me the shortcuts I had to make. I met men like Maeketsa, Samuel Mbiza, and a few more, and they gallantly showed me the cheats to survival, which are no cheats, but ways I did not see. They spoke to me about being obedient to the masters, active, participating and studying. That did try to help.

But I was still getting low marks and was at the peak of getting to repeat the Chemistry module. I was daily depressed and hourly perplexed. One time, when some love of a strange thing has already done loading in me, I just suddenly changed my mind-set. It was towards the conclusion of the academic year. I just got the mind-set of passing and getting the degree at any cost. I spoke to the friends immediately and said that I am going to get the degree by force.

That moment there, right at that moment, a clothing brand was conceived. A clothing business was being sharpened. I repeatedly spoke of "by force" to a point where I wanted what I speak to be printed in clothing. I spoke more about it, that one of my colleagues, classmate and friend heard me and volunteered to draft a logo for me. Then, the idea was developed. I had little doubts, because what I was having in mind was too big and new, especially to the family. I never met, nor saw someone who owns a clothing brand. I never even heard them speak. It was shocking and flabbergasting to me.

My dearest friend, Mr. Leave Mabegoane, gave me three samples of logos as the year was setting, and I asked few people in my WhatsApp chats, and I compiled the highest liked logo and sent it back to Leave to finish it up. At that moment, I fell in deep love with the brand. I loved it with almost all of me. I had big love for it, willing to do anything to see it in shops. He delayed a bit due to final exams and few other things, while at that moment, I already found a clothing printing station, and took my saved money and printed one shirt.

To tell the truth as it is, it was odd to my eyes. I had all the reasons to drop this thing and live a normal life, because I felt like what I was to start was very abnormal. I was used to getting clothes already printed, and now I buy a plain cloth and print it. That was very weird. I was wearing the shirt, but I was not so comfortable in it. I was thinking about the little ticket at the back of the shirt being printed #ByForce too. Surprisingly, people who saw me in the shirt really liked it.

Even so, I still did not feel normal. It was like I was faking myself or something. But that challenge from within, did not stop me, because the push was also from within.

So, since I long fought that inside friction, the outside ones were small waters to jump. I started printing few shirts of my own and went to Limpopo Province villages wearing my brand. They showed more love about it more than I thought. Even people who hated me said they want to buy it. I had to think about prices, which I had to think of production costs first and then charge. That's where my beloved clothing business started. I met quite many challenges in a single month, as it was being born and growing. As you read, it is in over three Universities in South Africa, worn by students. So, you might be wondering, where does religion get in here.

Well, in this brand, we have a #ByForce logo on the left chest, and a Biblical verse at the back. That is where business and religion meet, but never mix. The brand is more skewed to the business side, since when I speak of religion, you can take even a year before you can mention it, but when speaking of businesses, you will remember it sooner or later.

The religion part of it was caused by the market we aimed, seeing that the brand was for mostly formal clothes, and most formal wearers are church goers. So, we had to put something at the back to make them love the brand. And in that, we found the opportunity to preach to nations without saying a single word. I would enter a shop wearing one of my shirts, brand, with a verse behind, and someone would like to take it a picture, so they can read the verse at home since it comforted them instantly at that moment. But I cannot say the brand is a religion, no, water is not oil. They met but did not mix.

I am glad in this business I met well equipped brothers. When? I first took in Michael Mbhalathi, I liked him for his knowledge of business, and the fact that we are from common faith. I hope you remember him, the young man I just shared with you. The one who sells at schools with his mom. Yes, he is having a position in my brand business. And he is very key and very categorical. Another brother I have, from the tutoring company we started, Tshwarelo Gerald Matinketsa, very dedicated and smart too, is a key tool to the brand business.

Because I love the brand, I did not want to put liabilities to it, but assets. And I do not regret having invited the two of them into being co-founders of the #ByForce brand. They are useful. They assist in growing this baby with me, as they say that a child is raised by the whole community. There is always that few groups that are closest to it, and those are the three of us.

Business and religion are two different worlds, which touch, rub, but when mixed, they are poisonous. You can look at the religious leaders who have turned their conclaves into business. People suffer there. And being business minded, it is good to do what they do, but evil in the side of a religious person. Business does not care who is hurt if it can be fed and be full. Sadly, it eats every day, and like a grave, its stomach is never full. I can pitifully look at the followers of a business religious leader, who only cares about his pocket than the health, needs and well-being of the followers. It is evil to have that, so evil.

That is the evil that is involved in business, and until you have that evil in you, you might not succeed in business. It is rare to succeed without the demons of business. It is very rare to become a successful businessperson without the evil of business. The evil of business, which is not to care a lot about people, but business first. If a person benefits the business, they are welcomed and cared for, if they do not, they are chopped off and overthrown.

I do not say you cannot succeed in business until you start cunning people, no, or start mixing business and religion, no, but I speak of putting your business first. If your business comes first, that is evil to humanity, since every business hurt someone somewhere, either with resources, emotionally (Which I really do not care of), physically or economically. In business, having the evil of it is to put it first, and people last. Once you put people first and business second, you have lost your business. Because it is in the desire of people to gain a lot from business, and in so doing, they suck it to death.

But if you put business first, then you will suck the people wisely so, by giving them little and taking lot, you will have a well-fed business. It is evil, yes, to humanity. But is it not true that what is evil to a springbok is not evil to a lion? In business, it is good to attract people to come and use their money, you only want that which they have, and you give them what you have. In that exchange, to be good in business, you must be getting more than you give.

I have said a lot of things, let me just sit back a bit and excavate the idea of business and religion.

There is business in religion, and there is religion in business. What I see being lesser evil to humanity is the religion in business. Because business in religion is when the organization you run is more based on business, more skewed to the business side and more focused on business than religion, but still making it all look like is religion. It is like someone who has an initial idea of making money and think of religion as a perfect spot for making money. So, the religion started because of money, and for money. All the activities in that religious organization will be with the aim of making money, not for religious help. That is more evil and wicked. It is inhumane, but in business it is very good, because it is business after all.

Then there is religion in business. That is quite ok, it is lesser evil, and it is what my brand is all about. There is an idea on business, and you find a way to raise it up, then, put religion inside, as a form of market, respect, honor or giving back to the community. The business in this way, it can fully run without involving religion, but it becomes a choice for putting it in. Like with #ByForce. Do you think it will not run without verses at the back? It is having hats, and they do not have verses, business happen and run smoothly so. Unlike with business in religion, where if you take out religion, the business has fallen. It is like the business is climbing a horse, and that horse is religion.

Whereas, without religion in/on business, the religion is climbing a horse, and the horse is business. With an example of a book printing station. It is a business, not religion. So, should the owner decide to expand business, they can start printing Bibles and selling them. In that way, it is religion on business.

Since I see business as being evil to humanity, but having a variety of evil, where somewhere there is lesser evil and somewhere there is eviler, I like to dwell in lesser evil, because I still care for my people. Hence even the Scriptures allude that the love of money is the root of all evil. That is business. Remember what I said, you cannot have a successful business if you do not love it, and loving it is actually loving what it gives, which is mostly money, and hence, loving money is the root of all evil. Where the evil differs, there is higher evil, where people are in the business of killing people, selling them, enslaving them, and torturing them. That is business, they love it, yes, and it is good to their eyes, but wickedly evil to humanity. Then there is lesser evil, where you only take people hard worked results, and even if a person starves to death, you do not give them anything from the business, until the business gains from that.

Many wonders at billionaires who call media when giving back to the community the business is gaining more than what they give away. That is still evil. They are avoiding paying more tax, by giving little, and people jump over that. If they were losing for giving away, their business would have fallen and died long ago. That is the evil of all these businesses, but it is lesser evil. And can even be regarded as no evil at all. But still evil anyway since there is a depreciation to something of another human.

Chapter Four

Downfall of Business

Since we have already looked at religion and business, now I have more gut to write about how many businesses fall. Do not think it is because of religion since I write like this, no. It is because I have mentioned few things under that topic, which really do count a lot to a business falling. One of those things is when putting people first and business last. That is a slow poison to every business. In business there is no Samaritan. No, there is no friend. No. Good businessmen and businesswomen are those who are cursed on daily basis by people who want free things. Once you are good to humanity while you are in business, I tell you, you have lost that business. It might fall after a year, a month or even decade, but falling is its destination.

Religion will teach you well, that if you give, you get, but sadly in business, we do not just give without getting anything we already calculated back. If so, that means it is not just business, but you took your cut from the business and gave it to religion, and got a lot of money, then fed the business. Business does not go to church; business knows no god and business has no ancestors. Business is business, it only cares about now more than yesterday and tomorrow. And friends of a businessperson are those who sacrifice for the well-being of that business, not the persons who give as much as they equally gain. A good friend in business is the one who buys and says keep the change. That is a friend, while the rest are customers.

Should you say Kamohelo paid with extra money yesterday, and today you give him more product, you have lost a business. Some people claim to run businesses while they are not, because they are busy giving back to the community without receiving anything in return. Soon they could no longer give back because they are sucked to death. Business and people are like a bird and a tree, they need each other but toxic to one another somehow.

A bird needs a tree to survive, and a tree needs a bird to spread and survive its genes, also for strong growth from decomposed matter of a bird. The other gains at the loss of others. The tree gains more from the bird when the bird is dead and decomposed, while the bird gain more from the tree when the tree is being eaten, burdened, and used for sleep. But somehow, there is a balance in nature.

People and business do need each other and are toxic to one another. When a person is glad for having gained more than they were supposed to, it is the business that suffers at that time. When the business is glad for having gained more than it was supposed to, it is the person that suffers. The business that gives free things to people, most of the time it is not losing, provided it is aiming at attracting more people. Like a crocodile that tires itself by standing still, to pretend to be dead, so that some prey can come, with the goal of preying on the dead-living crocodile. It is always a win situation to a well-planned and structured business. Because to run a good business, some good planning is needed.

To give you an instant where a business can give away free product, let's say a certain business is dying, and found by a wise businessman at the point of death. Then the man notices that people do not like the business. So, he simply calculates the profits and costs, and prepares to lose the profit of a month, and give customers free goods when they buy. In that way, the heart of a person is trapped, the person will start to love the shop, and will not hesitate to come back. Out of all people who have been given free products, more than half are likely to come back to the shop next time and buy, so, the business will likely make more profit than it lost.

But a foolish businessman will just instantly give away products without a calculation and end up opening a wound in the business which cannot be closed. That's the downfall of it. Proper planning is needed for every decision and action taken, especially financial planning. Because finances are the blood of every business, they are the ones flowing around the body of business to transport duties and ideas. Lawyers might be needed for good legal advice, what do you need? Money. Well, an argument can be proposed, where one can say connection is needed rather, well, that might be true, but that would be fraud against oneself, since connections are not inheritance that can be left to the upcoming generation, but finances and possessions can.

As it can take thirteen years to raise a teenager, but few seconds to destroy it. Likewise, it can take ages to raise a business, but few decisions to destroy it. Bad decisions wound the business, and good decisions bind wounds and grow the business. It is good businesspeople who make good decisions on business. What kind of decisions are these? How can one see if they made a good decision? Well, you notice by the impact it has on the business. If you hired a person who is well spoken in the field of the business you offer, and they do help a bit, but consume more funds of the business, that the monthly turn-over starts decreasing, with no foreseen remedy to rise it up, that was a bad decision.

Some strong businesses fall and die due to resistance to change with times. Surely as you cannot crack a new business with old tricks, so is it that you cannot keep a business running with old methods. Many businesses died due to the resistance to change and due to the viscosity to the times. A business is a person remember, it needs new ideas, and it needs to flow with fashion. It might forgive you for introducing it a bit late to every fashion that enters to every era, but do not deny it the ability to grow.

Imagine a person who still anoints themselves with dung, like those of old, while people use lotions. Having passed from dung to lipids, from lipids to vegetable oil, from that to Vaseline, to more sophisticated Vaseline, and then lotions, yet someone is still stuck in dung. They will die from the society, not because they do not want the society, but because the society will no longer want such a person nearer.

A business that does not move with times, is slowly depreciating to its grave. It is plotting a grave number, and to tell the truth, graveyards of businesses are flooding. If you get a chance to cruise around many villages, you will not pass many streets without passing an old building which looks like an old dead shop. There were many reasons why such businesses died, but one of the few common reasons is the resistance to changing with times.

The owners still wanted to serve customers the old way, when the society was living the new way. Some businesses were having those old telegrams, selling woods and exes. Then when the society was moving to cell phones, coals and stoves, the businesses which survived are those which did away with woods, and started selling coal, then later electricity tariffs.

Do not let your business collapse in front of you; try at least to move with times, and one way to do that is by researching and becoming a lifelong learner. Hearing from your customers, on what they like and how. That is another trait that have killed some businesses. The denial to listen to customers. The golden rule in business that says the customer is always right did not just come by mistake.

It was the one to address the matter of listening to customers. If the business really wants the customer to buy, then it must listen to what the customer wants, and how. Many businesses that do that, which have turned into servants of customers, they are well succeeding. They seem to be too obedient to some customers. Imagine you enter a shop to buy airtime voucher, and they ask you how you would like it to be, the omni-network one, or closely specific one. To your eyes it might seem like they are joking or something, but after having asked 100 customers, and 80 wanted the omni-network voucher, he then changes his vouchers to omni-network.

Another unfortunate trait that I noticed, which collapses many gigantic businesses is greed. Especially when the business is multi-owned. If three people come together and opened a business together, it might seem like they might have done it individually, but the reason it would reach whatever level it will reach. It will because of the unity and division of duty in a short space of time. So, amongst them, one might be greedy, and act foolishly so. He might start making decisions alone, involving more of his family members or even assassinating the other members.

Such have a potential of dropping a business at its knees. Yes, some businesses have gone through such and are still breathing, but few businesses have been buried because of such reasons. Greed, it creates ideas which feed the individual and potentially consume the business. Remember, when you open a business, you do not like it to fall, and when you have a running business, you do not want to witness its downfall. So, to ensure there is no downfall of business, you take as many precautions as possible, and that is by listening to few folks speak.

Always worry about the business more than the person, that is one way to keep it up and moving for a long time. Anyway, remember that the business can run for a millennium of years, but a person does not. So, if you care for a person who cannot even reach 1000 years living, why don't you just care for the business which can live forever? If it can be well planned, even for the future, and for the change that arises in the future, then it can run. Look at businesses like Smirnoff; are its founders still alive?

No, from 1818 until now they are long gone. Look at these old brands, their founders died long ago, but the business is still well and alive. It is not because it fell into the right hands, but because it was started and planned by right hands. The hands that found it, found it well and alive, and labored to keep it running, by helping it adjust with times.

Or maybe you think Micro-soft is still giving out products which it used to give 10 years ago? No, though the man who started it died, but it should respect change in times and stay strong and alive. One of the things that brings the downfall of businesses is the involvement of politics inside. Politics alone are toxic; they are parasitic on their own. So, imagine bringing them to the stomach of your business. You are killing it, destroying it pejoratively so.

Every business is being daily and perpetually scratched from the outside, by people who are not in it. That is normal, it is a must be. But when the business is being scratched by the ones inside it, it will have wounds which no stitch can reach. It would be having stomach cramps which no hand can reach for healing. The troubles outside the business grow it, but the ones from the inside kill it. Another blinding issue that silently assassinates a corporate is the act of personally giving money to the business, to fund it continually, and being convinced that the business is having healthy finances, when it is you giving it the fact alarms. As the saying goes, that you should not give a man a fish, but teach him how to fish. So, with business, you do not give it finances perpetually, but program it, teach it how to fish, and it will fish. In that fishing, it is the people who shall be fish.

Giving money to a business will be like a make-up on the face of a corpse, it will look good for a moment, if the make-up lasts, but will decompose sooner or later. You cannot call an organization that has no profit as business. In business, profit is breath, and the money is blood. Without two, the business is dying. Without breath, it will suffocate, and can reach a point of collapse. Take care of the business in a manner that is wise.

Why does it seem like the only way to make a business succeed is when someone else loses something? Well, yes, that is the only way. Either you lose for a moment, or forever. Just like an investor in those big businesses, they might lose for a moment, or forever. If it is for a moment, they will soon gain, while someone somewhere is losing. It is like that. Because I take the value of money as energy, you cannot create it, and you cannot destroy it as a business. So, you ought to get it from somewhere, and that somewhere must be losing it. There is no money tree to the business universe, so, it must be earned. And the earning of it, someone is losing something. The business might be giving away what it produces, but it is focused on the money.

A business that focuses on giving out best quality of the product without looking at its finances is like a person having blind folded themselves and walk in a forest. They will hear of danger, but not see it because they do not want to see it, yet sooner or later, will experience it with the expense of their health. Be vigilant in business. As I said, do not be too wicked to humanity, but rather should you be too kind. Even the Holy Scriptures tell us that we should not be too wicked, and not too righteous because by doing so we destroy our own selves.

If one has a generous heart, in business they are an enemy. If one has the heart of giving continually, in business, they are an assassinator. Do not deprive your character of being good to humanity though, you can get your own cut from business and give away, not the business money, but your money from the business. Business cannot fish and then take back the fish to the sea.

The downfall of business is in many ways; hence a vigilant businessman and businesswoman is needed to lead a business. To be able to see everything that can cause change to the business, either media, economy, society, place around it, or any other thing that can cause either a bad change or a good change to the business. You must be able to see such, foresee them if it is needed, and act. Ensure the negative things to the business are prevented, like bad debts, bad leadership, and bad position. You cannot place a clothing business near a place where there are plenty clothing businesses unless the place is overcoming the other clothing businesses by demand.

Also ensure that the positive things are gladly and cautiously accepted to the business. To deny good things to happen to the business, like the ceasing of an opportunity to open a new branch, is denying the growth of the business. One more thing that brings businesses to a downfall is fear and lack of courage.

Sometimes the business needs the push by force spirit for it to continue walking. It needs the „We Must do it" spirit for it to run. So, use force if it's needed, just to keep it moving, or make it grow.

Chapter Five

Evil Of Business

We must know that sometimes a business can be right to people, but not always good. For many things can be good, and not right and some can be right and not good. Well, it is better to have something that is right and not good, than to have something that is good and not right.

Being good is when it is feeling right to do and being right it is when it is influencing and resulting into more right. Being good is like stealing from other shops, with the aim of making only your business stand, but is that right to do? No. Businesses do need each other. There must be some competition between them. A child in school without competition will think they are best, yet to only know later that there are three times smarter kids than them in another school. The competition in business should be embraced, not demarcated.

So, what further evil can we say there is in business? It is quite a topic we cannot exhaust discussing, since the fact that business survives at the loss of someone, then, that is evil on its own. It is like how a lion survives; it survives at the loss of one of the springboks. But that is already normal to us, but it is evil. Yet, that is the kind of evil we can only watch, and not try to stop, because once we stop, we have started the extinction of one of the species. We should just know how much evil business is, so that if you start a business, you should not feel ashamed to do such good evil to humanity. It is a paradox indeed.

But without argument, there is some evil of business which should not exist, just like when a lion dines on a living prey, eating it while alive. That kind of evil should not be experienced. It is like the kind of evil in business where not only people's financial life is depreciating, but also their lives and physical health is at stake. That is pure rebarbative evil. See a person who does a business on religion and try to get the members to buy certain unnecessary goods for the sake of gaining finances, regardless of the health of the people. Like making people eat rats in church, and psychologically having programmed them, that if they give money, they will not notice.

Look at religious leaders who make poor members pay big money for services. That is not religion; it is rather business in religion. And the religion part is not evil, what is evil is the business part of the religion. Because business does not care about the well-being of the people, but its own well-being.

Having to sell oil to the congregation at a very high price and promising them things which might not come to pass.

Yes, we try to understand that the church is trying to raise funds, but unfortunately it has employed business to come and make funds for them. I do not recall the old church in Scripture cunning people to bring finances to the church. Look at how the leader of the religious business will be wealthy in a short period of time, living in lavish while congregants live in anguish. That's pure evil and parsimonious evil. Many views religious business as evil and some uncritically and illogically conclude that religion is evil, no, it is not, business in religion is the one that is evil. It is pulverizing the society bit by bit.

Many might hate to read and hear what is here, but I cannot be scared to state the truth because of being scared to lose the audience magnitude. I rather choose to be a person who spit out the truth and have few speakers, than to lie to many and gain their ears. Anyway, many people would like to hear what they already know, and do not want to learn anything new, are you such a person? If you are, then there is nothing new that you have learned for a while, and cannot learn anything else, because learning cause change to a person.

Change is a result of learning. To show that you have learned something from Grade 8 to Grade 12, you have drastically changed, so humongous. So, should you deny new knowledge and new reasoning, then there will be no learning. Anyway, knowledge without work is a carcass, it can do nothing but rotten the attitude and behavior.

Knowledge without wisdom is like having petrol but no car to put it in, it cannot become useful, because I view wisdom as being the ability to logically use knowledge, which then makes me want to enter philosophy a bit, which is the love of wisdom. What I present to you, is philosophy in a way, because here I bring forth knowledge which I then use logically so and pay around with it together with reasoning. To say business is evil, in philosophy that can only be correct or wrong according to how I substantiate it.

I hope thus far, I have pejoratively given explicit reasons, which I am still willing to give furthermore, since the topic content is in excess, and time is a limiting reagent here.

Business becomes eviler when its existence is in the cost of lives and not just their financial health. If the gain of the business is causing death to humanity, then its existence is unacceptably evil. Not like the mortuary business, that one does not cause death, but take care of the dead, there is a difference there. Businesses like drug businesses, those ones are a curse to humanity, because the person running it is indeed glad that the business is growing, and it is healthy growing indeed, but at the expense of permanent damage to humanity. Taking someone's money is not permanent, but for a moment, but taking their lives or even physical health, in the goal of trying to grow the business, that is eviler than a lion eating a prey alive.

As business is evil anyway, saying that from the perspective of me as a person, the evil varies, it is different from one proportion to another. The business that injures the financial health, while giving something in return, that is goodly evil, since the person is temporarily scratched and got something in return of the scratch. But a business that takes anything outside finances from customers, that is wicked, and some that take finances but does not return good satisfying quality back to the people, it is likewise evil.

Having been a Samaritan and started a business, I have continually felt guilty for when the people lose and I gain, but that was in the view of the matter as a human being, when viewed as a businessman, I gladly proceeds the trade and even will to grow the business, that is, to make as many people as possible to lose their money, while they gain my good product.

That is clearly business, it is evil, I can feel it, though few do feel what I feel, because those ones are genuine businessmen and businesswomen, but I also do cease the feeling when I see the smile of a customer gladly accepting my product.

Another attractive evil that is done by business on humanity is what I solely call cornering-and-attack (CAN). This is where a business creates a problem in the society, in such a way that the society will be forced to move to a single corner, and then the business come as a helping aid, and gain from there.

Look at internet, which is a good example. It has created a problem of making people feel like without it they are worthless, especially the youth of this generation; they vividly cannot live without internet. They can even wish water to flee, if they have internet, they are well. And, having created that problem, it then comes as tries to solve that problem, where the ones being helped are losing some finances to gain access to internet. In like manner, the business is gaining and growing more at the expense of the people. Can't you see that this is evil too? Because it corners the people, putting them in a position where they cannot move unless by the business, and in so doing, they lose and the business gain.

Now, in schools, assignments and assessments need internet to go on, if not, a person would fail and go back home. That is evil, is it not so? But it is the evil that is entailed in business. To business it is so good, healthy, but to humanity it is flagitious. Another instance of trying to excavate the CNA is by looking at the health industries. In this one, I do not have all full proof to state, but I will just let it pass by your ears. I do not wish to put forth thesis which have no reasoning. In the health business, if the business is not going well, it is very good for the business to create a problem, which is creating a certain disease or virus, which will shock humanity and corner them, so that they are forced to come running to the health industries. In such a way, the health business is gaining and growing, but at the sudden expense of the people. That can be more wicked, when such a virus reaches an impoverished person, who do not afford to feed the health business what it needs in exchange to get back his health. This is inimical and inhumane. Anyway, business is not humane, but an inhumane person.

Yet, during the creation of the virus, the people's health is neither an idea nor a concern, but money is and people's money. Its value, since money alone is just paper, its value is its power. One of my dearest friends and brother in various common grounds, Briton Mbhiza, he said it nakedly, that in winter, the tree is dry and depends on its roots to stand against harsh storms. That is so true also in business, since during dry season of the business, the customers have fled the scene, the business depends on its roots, which is evil to humanity" for it to stand against the fall. Look at the case that once happened, but was caught and dealt with by human agents, where a biscuit producing company was falling, and it decreased the magnitude of biscuits in each pack, without decreasing the mass gage, and the price. Only the size inside, such that if three packets are decreased, they can make up another new packet. That was so evil, that was the „evil to humanity" nature of a business, which it depends in its roots for survival.

Looking at the business that sells fat cakes to people, during summer, it is in a dry season, and close to falling. Then, it can use its roots, which is „evil to humanity" to rise again. It can start producing fancy fat cakes that are accompanied with soft drinks, just to keep the business moving, and use as much advertisement to fish for people. This is clearly the „evil to humanity" root of the business, since the fat cakes are not healthy to people in summer, since a lot of lipids would generate, causing more depreciation to the health of the people. But to the business, this is the only way to stand against the fall, using its roots.

Look at another business that tries to keep itself up and running during a dry season, and adds water to the product they sell, just to try and increase the magnitude of products, to gain more finances. But we can agree here that this would be more than evil since it will be deceiving people. One instance is when the Corona virus pandemic hit the Globe, there the business of sanitizers was held by the scrotum by demands. So, many businesses added water to the concentration of the sanitizers, to try and gain more cash than usual. That is evil. One can argue the case of increasing the prices that as demands go high, the sales also proportionally increase. But isn't that evil? To see that more people are coming to buy, and you increase the sales. That to the business world is very good. Hence even in the school of business, they advise to increase prices of sales when demands go high. It is good to business since if it does not increase sales, the products might be finished sooner, and having missed the opportunity of making more cash.

Some businesses fail by disobeying what a successful businessman said, Bill Gates, that he does not miss any opportunity. Many businesses will gain less when they had the ability to gain more, and they didn't take that opportunity. Is not business evil? So why feel bad when sales must be increased when demands increase? That is how the business survives.

It is not hard to be a Christian and a businessperson, what is hard is complying to the rules and roots of business. When a hungry person comes to your business, and you must choose which hat to wear, the Christian hat or the business hat. The two can meet and live together for a very long time, but never mix. I am a Christian and a businessman. When it comes to business, unfortunately I must forget that I am a Christian, hence I do feel guilty at some points. Not because I am robbing people or cunning them. No, just doing the usual and legal business, but because it is evil to humanity, I feel that guilt. Yet, I must just put on the business hat and proceed with the growth of the business.

To see further how business is, look at the man that is hungry for business, they will do anything at their disposal to plant the business and water it with the sweat and blood of people's financial health, by any cost, more evil or less evil to humanity, just to get that business up and fruitful. And notice that a business does not just bear fruits when it just has been planted. It will need to be watered with ideas, finances, and leadership for it to grow, and then it can stand on its own and be able to give back the fruits. Which have the capability to provide seeds to plant other businesses.

Let me recall another brother of mine in common faith and business, Johannes Segooa, a hard-working young man. He is a wide viewing man who would cease any pleasuring business idea. He has a media company, and few other companies. But sadly, I will be sharing the failing side of us in business, because we are ghostly business partners. When we completed Grade 12 together, having been from the same class, we had the ambition to give back to the community. We had ideas, and I love him for the energy to execute ideas. So, we planned a business amateurly so, and registered a Non-
Governmental Organization, with the name of The Lord's Servants Youth Foundation. In that organization, we planned to get sponsors and give back to the community, by doing community service and assisting youth with as many resources to them being independent adults. What made that a business, was the fact that we planned to gain from such a service? But sadly, such a business fell right at our faces.

What made it fall was not the lack of love for it alone, but also the lack of information. Because we moved without knowledge of many things, we were blindly moving, we did not research enough. We wanted to access the business planet without being evil. I did not know that business can be evil to people, hence, I used as much energy to cease the evil from happening to humanity, but in so doing, I cut the roots of a tree and expected it to grow.

There are two sides of people when comparing business and humanity. There are those who love springbok so much, that they do not want anything to happen to it, and then there are those who love lions so much, that they do not want anything to happen to it. Will you believe me when I say, the two are enemies without knowing. Because when the person who loves lions observes a hungry lion, they will seek to kill a springbok, and feed the dying lion. In so doing, that would hurt the person who loves springboks. That is purely business and humanity. Business survives when humanity loses. But lesser evil is when the business survives when humanity gain little and lose more. Once humanity gains more and loses less, the business is dying of hunger, and needs someone who cares for it, to come and kill a prey for it.

I hope I have now shown you that business is evil. But the evil is good somehow, depending on how evil it is to humanity. By now you should be able to conceive a business idea, develop it with information and more love for it, and give birth to it. Once it is born, you should be able to feed it with right food, for it to grow stronger, until it becomes an independent person, where it can fully run even without your presence. You must be able to notice the roots of a business and take the seed of business you have in mind, one that you love and plant it, water it, nurture it and allow it to grow. Do not try to expect fruits from it when it just grew, develop it further, directing it to the direction you would like it to bend it when it is still young. And then allow it to reach that state of giving back fruits, allowing it to give birth to other businesses.

By now, you should be able to begin a business from scratch, feed it with right material and plan, nutrients which I have mentioned. And not try to milk it before it can develop fully, but wait for it, embracing its youth, not undermining it for being small. But, vigorously fighting for it to reach that state of being milked and feeding many. For if it is not milked, then, then one who will milk it (Tax), will leave no evidence of the milk, but will consume it all.

Business is evil, yes, but a need to people, since from its existence, empires are built and ones which last from generation to generation. Start a business, and remember to care about it more than humanity, but in that process, do not forget that you are also part of humanity. No matter how small you start, remember to do small while thinking big. Cease every opportunity to grow. Do not be scared to fail, for failures are learning elements to succeeding and being perfect next time.

Chapter six

The rich and the poor

Many might ask why I write about rich people and poor people inside business, how they are included in this kind of world. Some might even ask further at why I write about the rich when I have never experienced how it is to be rich, well, let me just share with you what I know, and the rest you can learn with other authors and sesquipedalian in the business cosmos.

What I know about the rich and the poor is that business is a big contributor to the classification of mankind. Business is the one able to make the poor even poorer, and the rich richer. Some might argue and say the economy or other factors are the ones doing that, but you should not leave business outside when counting factors responsible for separating mankind into two major classes. Anyway, that is another kind of evil of business, the ability to make someone be viewed as nothing, because they are poor.

What rich mean to me is that it is the ability to afford the needs and get the wants anytime. A rich person can get anything they want, though time might limit depending on how rich they are.

The poor to me means someone who cannot afford, someone who struggle to even buy the very need. Someone who cannot manage to pay for electricity, because it was not a need, but now because of business as I already alluded, electricity has become a need. You cannot attend well at school without internet, especially higher institutions. It is sad on how these things are done by what was started by men, but there it is. The poor cannot manage to buy what they need, though they might see, but business need to gain some finances from the person, where in turn, business will provide what is needed by the person.

The poor tend to remain at a poverty level, succumbing to the depression caused by business. Where a person will only work for a certain business, it pays them very little; they take the very same change back to the business for living, for the needs, for raising children. Just literally working for the needs and struggling in doing so. Because we are surrounded by business, I do not care small or big, registered, or unregistered, but we do work with business around. Business is just all around us. When you want something, you get it through business, from a business or by business. There are very rare things you get outside the business world, especially in towns.

They will tell you that nothing is for free, which means there must be gain on both sides, just that the business usually consumes more than it gives. Some poor like to remain at the lower level of the business chain, where they just toil for survival. They cannot get what they wish for, but only what they are compelled by survival needs to get them.

They work, and spend all, work and spend all, without saving, investing, or even pursuing a way of elevating them from the lower part of the business chain. They do not want to at least start a little business, or save some money for property, but they spend all their earnings even before the middle of the month. That to me is sore poverty, lack of high order. No plan for life, just waking up to work, struggling in transport because they want the cheapest way to work, work, struggle to eat at work, come home, find something to eat back home, sleep, wake up and the same circle revolve just in one place.

Some sadly even their children fall to the same circle, and they love it. That is some sort of slavery, localized in serious places, where it would take passion, dedication and sacrifice to pull out of that circle. And it is only through business that they can make it out legally. Some steal, they would plan a big gig of stealing and then stop stealing, just to access finances to break the circle. Some succeed, but many are destroyed in that mission.

The poor are best at spending. If you notice, a lion will go to live near a place where there are many springboks. So, also with business, it noticed that many poor people like spending, and it lodged near them. Count how many shops are there in townships, in every street, I bet with you, in every street they sell something. Those who opened those businesses, many of them do not live there, they live in areas they wished for and got, and brought their business to come and milk the people in the township areas, because there are many poor people. People whose profession is spending money.

Some by beer, where if you calculate, they spend more money than what it takes to build one room in just a month yet living in a rented house. Cigarette have been made fashion, where many smokes more money than someone's monthly payment into a car they drive, but the one smoking is only a learner or having few shoes. It is sad from the human point of view, very sad. But from the business view, it is super, because that is what it needs, for people to spend money. Many rich people are rich by business, so, they delight in the agony of others as they lose finances which grow that business.

Poor people save money to celebrate holidays, parties and so forth. They would make a celebration out of anything. If there are seven children in the house, they would spend a lot seven times a year only on birthdays. Every year. One person saving the whole eleven months, just to spend it all in one month, December. Through those holidays. In December they look all rich, spending like there is no next year, but during the year some are poor than dogs of ministers.

They do not save to invest, but to spend. The poor save money for celebrations of no victories; the rich save money for investment, and then celebrate victory in business. What they spend in celebrations is far less scratching their bank accounts. Look at this, I am not saying you should not celebrate, no, do not get me wrong. What I am saying is that rise first, and then celebrate.

Do not celebrate Youth-Day every year without any proper progress in your life. Skip celebrating it for three times, five times, investing and see how same you will never be after investing smartly so. Never rush quick cash, because it works for few, and demolish many. Like with the foreign exchange, it is quick money to some, hence over 80% of traders lose tons of money. They fall from that little investment to the depth of poverty. Then, to notice that a poor man enjoys poverty, they are slaves of lamentation, they would want shows on Television which will show people who lost many amounts of money in just few moments.

Start investing now and forget the celebrations which whoever you celebrate does not know you. Rather celebrate later, knowing that even if you take out money to braai for the whole community, that will just scratch your bank account balance. And never make the mistaken mentality of saying, what if you die before eating your investments? That is the mentality of a poor man, because they resist to go out of that circle, they enjoy it. They like working for survival and celebrating same thing repeatedly with only age and poverty going up. Break those chains, start spending less on things which cannot return the money. At the age of 20, I started telling myself that I want to spend on what will return more money to me.

Yes, there are things like bread which do not directly bring back the money, but I get energy from there to hustle more. Thus far I am involved in many organizations, looking for any chance I can get to flee the poverty chain of my family, like a guy who is looking forward into leaving country and has no money for transport, he would try to catch any transport leaving the country, might work a short period for that person or so forth. I am not speaking of illegal immigration; I speak of missioned legally transportation.

You will catch any transport that can take you there. Like in the rural areas, where you wait an hour for a single taxi to town, you do not choose the beauty of the car, but catch any that goes to town. Should you wait for the beautiful one, you might spend little bit more time without going anywhere. I get into any that might take me to where I wish to go to, for my mind-set and mentality have been changed, I can feel that I no longer belong to the chains of the poor, I have a rich mind-set now. Investing any cent, the one I have positively, in any organization that is promising, feeling pain when I lose even a single second without doing anything.

I refuse to remain in the land of our poor ancestors for long, let me go and get gold for those who remain, and bring them up too, by giving them content which will change their mind-set. Because I can foolishly give them money to start businesses without them having a converted mind-set, then I have wasted money, because it would be spent like there is no tomorrow.

Like the older parents who left villages to Gauteng the city of gold, they left their poor parents in search for gold, and some did return and built houses for their parents. That is why we are still poor, because they came back and gave us minerals, making the body rich but the mind still poor. So, not to repeat that same mistake, there will be a need to change the mind-set first. And if you notice, even the level of talk between the rich and the poor differs. The rich discuss events, ideas, plans, investments, negotiations, but the poor discuss others, they discuss the calamities, compering who is poorer among their own poverty, discussing how others do all day long, weeklong. Even at work, they tend to work discussing others. If John is out, they speak about him, giving each other names. Poor minds, poor deeds, speaking of nothing which will benefit them.

I do not think I am lying here, because I speak of what I see, what I witness, what I experience. I have set around the poor; I know their mind. They would sit from 9AM till 10PM discussing, but when each go to bed, there is nothing useful for their own growth to break chains which would have been discussed. Only soccer, on how Teko Modise is old and not good for football, or how Barcelona have lost the league, things which are not important to assist them in growing, but only keeping them more chained in the chain, in that circle of poverty. When a man changes positions, even his mind change.

Even in soccer, when a striker is called to be a goalkeeper, they will have to change the mindset, the talk, the behavior, the attitude. I am not speaking of soccer for fun, but this is to help you understand how to break through from poverty to wealth. From poor to rich. A striker thinks about scoring, when they get the ball, all they think is how to trick the keeper. The striker's mindset is to ensure they score, by any chance. But as for a goalkeeper, they want to make sure that there is not even one player which will score. Different positions, different mindsets. The striker speaks with those near him differently from how a keeper speaks with

defenders. That is, it. The poor think very different, act very different, talk very different from the rich. The poor entertain what keeps them still locked in poverty, while the rich entertain what unlock them even more. And if you notice, the poor are in control of nothing rather than their families, sadly some do not have families. They cannot even control their income, their time, they are commanded, and they obey the commands for survival.

While the rich control how much they should get, how much time they invest into certain things. When the poor are spending their time on a television, at that time, a rich man is spending time to ensure he brings the poor what they like, knowing he will get more from that. The poor would take 30 minutes watching a television drama, then the rich spend that 30-minute planning a pitch for a million.

Rands costing project to bring the next drama on show. That is the circle. The rich control, the poor follow. The rich are puppeteer; the poor are puppets, all because of business. If the rich want the poor to not watch a certain drama, they can change that anytime, by giving the poor little platform to chat, where they think they are in control, but the fact is, they are only giving the master ideas of where to turn the puppet to next. And it is all happening through business. The poor lose time and money into feeding a business that one rich man invested money to start, and it is growing humongous.

Then there is a gap I mentioned arbitrarily so, a gap between poverty and wealth, a gap between the poor and the rich. That gap is a process, where many get to, but sadly fall back to the poverty side. The gap requires ideas, intellectual strength, patience, sacrifice, investments, planning, understanding of where you are going, change of mentality for you to pass it to the other land. Some are poor minds living in rich bodies. Someone wins lotto, or gets inheritance, a flight from poverty to wealth many wish for but never get, and because this person has a poor mentality. The mentality of spending without the money coming back, they still think same as a poor man, they will soon be singing "I blew it", "I was once having this much", and so on.

A poor mind cannot live in a rich body for long, it converts the body. The mind has a tendency of converting the body. When you think poor, you tend to become poor. So, if you want to pass through the gap between poverty into the wealth land, you must change your mind-set, your mentality.

Amazingly so, there are rich minds in poor bodies, I tell you, those ones it is just a matter of time, the body will follow the mind-set. Once you start thinking like a rich man, you will become one. I am not saying you should start thinking of spending money a lot, buying expensive stuff without the way of getting that money back easily, then that is a poor mind, leading to a poor person.

I have seen people as I was growing, they worked at good paying jobs, which the rich decided to give more there, and those poor minds given more finances spent a lot, lived in lavish, but money somehow increase what you are, if poor, it tends to turn you even poorer. They spoilt their children into thinking spending is life. Now to reveal their poor minds, the job is over, and the body followed the mind. They are sore poor now. The babies are even poorer, since they grew knowing that spending without any easy way of making the money return is the only way to be happy.

These poor minds enforce their bodies to celebrate anything; they are people celebrating anything, even funerals. They call it "after-tears" where they buy beer and start spending. In all this, business is very happy and well. It is getting even more fat and fat, and soon will be having children too, which will feed on the finances of the children of the poor.

No matter how hard you convince a poor man about investing, they will always find a reason to spend. The mind-set is the problem. And how what you see, hear and smell influences your mind-set, is very amazing. Look at how business mastered that attribute of a poor man, on how to catch them well. They would show on media, people who spend their monies, without showing the hard work they put behind the work. That makes many poor minds think that spending is the only form of happiness.

Look at even school children, who amazingly can manage to save together, and hire a taxi, buy beers, because beer has been made look like is the only key to happiness, which is very false, they would even book a place where they can just go and celebrate the fact that they passed a certain Grade together. Like, how will such help in the future? It will just help with the talk, that when you completed Grade 12, you went to this place to celebrate, and this happened.

That is caused by how it was narrated to us, and now the children think is the only way to make history for yourself. That is a bad way, because it does not grow you in the future, it only grows topics which will enslave the minds of further generations. To believe in spending than earning. Just imagine if they saved together for an investment into a business, I know young guys who own studios, they saved for that.

If high school children can save for a trip, they can also save for a business. But sadly, the poor mind sees the other side better than this. It is both saving, but one will strengthen chains of poverty, while the other will break them. What if saving for December, you save and die before spending the money? If it happens, it happens is it not so? So, even with saving for investment, let it be so, if you die you will die, but die in the mission to break chains of poverty than to die perpetuating the strength of those chains. What if you do not save and then live longer?

You will wish you could have started saving today. But it would be too late. If you can save for a party, you can save for a project. Just that the poor have poor mentality, having ideas without passion. They give an excuse of having no resources, while they use the very same resources for happiness pursue. I was the second one at home who reached 21 years without having a baby, and according to the tradition of the poor, there should be a big party for me, where there would be a lot of spending, and saying they give me a key to adulthood or so forth, well, personally, as someone who is looking forward to breaking the chains, I refused the party.

I told them that they should not host it for me, not because I hate parties, but I hate spending without any earnings after that. This sounds mad to a poor mind, and good to a rich mind. Which one are you?

Chapter seven

Seventeen Rules of Business

One way of keeping a poor man even poorer, is to keep him enjoying that agony of poverty. It is to give him sweets while you have gold, to make them feel at home and free in that poverty, to think that they do not deserve to be rich, mental imprisonment.

The rich like the poor as poor as they are, because once he becomes rich, he becomes a threat to the rich, for it is not nice to share the wealth with strangers, the rich would ensure to entertain the poor in their poverty, so that they do not go much far to search for fun In their lives, they forget that they are poor, and lambast themselves into more depths of poverty. Look how malls are built near the poor and look at how the day of "Black-Friday" have been made happiness provider to the poor. They get happy to spend where things are said to be cheap, but in literal sense, things are just as they were.

Because there is still profit, meaning business still gains at the loss of men. That is how complex business can get, yet easy. So, to excavate business little bit deeper, let me give you some of the principles of business, rules which when followed, one is more likely to succeed in business. Because business is one of the best ways to break through the gap from poverty to wealth. These seventeen rules are not the only, but the few among many which govern the business world, they show nakedly how business run and go around.

These rules reasonably work for the success of business, and hence, even for the success in life. The first rule is "Never expect anyone to support you, even the close ones". This one work to keep your emotions intact. Because some people start businesses and rely on people close to them for support, and if they are not supported, they tend to think they are not enough or maybe not doing right, and perhaps get hurt at points. It is fair and safe to not expect anyone to support you, ask them to do, but do not expect them. Ask them as if you are just testing the waters, because some will say they can help, and not help by act but by empty promises.

Such have a potential of bringing you down. So, if you start a business and not expect anyone to help you, then anyone who would help you, appreciate them. Sometimes expecting people to do certain things might delay your business or decrease your passion when they cannot do as you expected them to. Expect less, do ask them to help, even when they help, do not expect much from them, just watch the action and success invested there by them. Even if they work good and smart, do not trust them or even expect them to be there forever, do not make any expectations, and you will be a happy man.

The Second rule is like the first one, it assists you in protecting your emotions, because once emotions are involved in business and they start being tarnished, you might lose direction. "Life doesn't owe you anything on Earth, appreciate anything good for business". And this is not limited to enemies. Your personal enemies can offer something which will be good for business, pride aside, appreciate it.

Never think someone owes you support, or help, they might owe you cents, but not support. Many young people do not pursue their ideas because they expected parents to support them, and when parents or family members do not support them, they tend to quit. Not good. So, to be safe, just know that even your own daddy does not owe you anything, any support, appreciate those who support you, anyone, even if it be parents. But if they support you, do not think they owe you, and must support you, no. If I should tell you, my own parents never supported me when I authored books, discouraged me, when I played rugby, they discouraged me, I even left it.

When I wrote poems and so forth, they do not owe me anything, so, I will not expect them to support me or even help me financially. I published books on my own, they might not even care, but, I know, they do not owe me anything.

The third rule is like the second one, it is like one thing, but there was a need for them to be separated like this. "Learn to support yourself, so you can support others". This might not be golden in business, but it counts, because it focuses on the business but also humankind. If you want to wait for someone to support you, you might not go anywhere. Start with your own funding. It is as rare as finding a walking snake, for one to receive funding for something they do not work toward. You will have to work hard for that idea of yours, so that soon you will be able to help others too.

When I speak of support, I speak of capital, start off, fan, stan, people who love your products, people who comment good, anything that is from someone which will bring a smile to your face is support, because it is giving you that emotional balance, which is called support, lest you fall. But if you do not get it, do it yourself. Support yourself, stan yourself, remember no one owes you, then support yourself. That investment I told you about, save for it. If you have a booming idea and you really *philo* it, you can save for many months, or even many years, just for that idea to happen. It is possible. I know of a friend, a brother by faith, who as I speak with you is saving money towards buying a little plot of land. He is studying farming at one of the universities, because he wants to be one. He is investing almost every cent. You might see him not celebrating holidays and wonder if he is poor, no, he is just a rich mind trapped in a poor body, but soon will be released.

His name is Khotso Ndowe, passionate about cows, goats, and livestock, just anything about farming. That is business too, just on its own. Hence, he needs to just proceed with that passion, being patient while investing, sacrificing. There are no many to support him, but he is supporting himself. Rather, many discourage him, but still, he follows the inner force, not the winds from outside. He stands on his roots, and just listen to the wind bending the branches. From our class teacher back at high school, to even the closest to him.

"Learn to use others, not abusively, but their resources, their knowledge, their ideas". Yes, almost a golden rule, because by it you rarely lose. When you master the art of using others, you tend to boom at what you intend to do. Instead of crying that you do not have resources you do have them around you, packed in someone's head. Ask around, you will notice you will learn more and grow. When I started looking for places where they print shirts, I looked for long alone, but after asking, I got it within hours. It is that easy. You just ask, and then that way you have rightfully used a person. Some they have a studio you might need for songs, use it.

But do not use the studio because the idea of songs came to you when you saw the studio equipment, that would be desire, which does not push a person far. Start having that passion first, then look around. As I told you, I never even thought of Nike and Adidas when I thought of HashtagByForce. I was just blank, and the idea came.

 I should tell you about someone I might not mention their name, who is good at using others. He would recruit people, as many as he can, and milk them the resources he needs, and then leave. I remember how I met him, it was through a certain brother in faith, then after a month, I noticed there was a fuse between them. But he kept me close by, even called meetings that we should start a church. Would even assist him on how to publish a book online for free. It was not for long when I noticed him since some people started leaving him.

He would use people's cars as if he hired them as his drivers. That kind of use is abusive. It is when you disregard the human nature and become sorely evil. That is not good, it is evil.

Though business be evil, but to some extent, the evil cannot be tolerated.

"Agree to be used, but never agree to be misused".
Connecting to rule four, this fifth rule is about you being the one used. Allow that to happen, because when you use someone, they gain something, and when they use you, you should gain something. It might be too little to notice, like just information that Peter is selling shirts now, next time you need to know more about it, you know where to go. And they might be willing to help, but remember rule number 1? Never expect them to help you, just go there as a try.

That is how I saw most Somalian shops flourish in South Africa, they grow very big and large, being ubiquitous. They support each other because they allow each other to be used. This type of rule is rare among poor minds, because what they want is to look good than others, to seem good when rotten inside. When you help others, by allowing them to use you, you expand your world. That is how connections begin. What you should drive home is; You can help them, but they might not help you sometimes. Though you are being used, know the limit, you should not be exploited, because that is what is done to poor minds, exploited. Do not be misused. The poor are used to grow many companies.

One scenario pained me, but it was good to someone's perspective due to the amount of truth it carries. One-time few workers of a company that got a new owner decided to work hard for their salaries to be increased, rather than complaining and putting their jobs at stake. Two months after they started working hard, their master bought a new car, but still no increase.

Further two months after they worked hard, the master bought a car for his wife. They toiled more, envying the master, even saying in their corners that they would like to get their salaries increased, so that they can even save for a car like the one of their master. But the more they toiled, the more the master bought cars, houses, farms.

Then one time one of the workers was brave enough during lunch and asked the master how he manages to be so successful in a short period of time. The master said the workers do a good job and work hard, so his business is making more profit than before, hence he manages to buy anything he wants. Such a case is fictional but real, just hidden in the closets to be said, but vivid to eyes. See how the poor are exploited to make the rich even richer? That is how they mastered the art of using others.

But now as a businessman, "You are the guard at the gate to your business", you choose who goes in or out. And do not be emotional when it comes to that, because once you are, you will end up keeping liabilities which are seating on the seats of assets. If something no longer makes profit for you, like a bouncer, take it out. As a businessman, you should not put family first in your business if they do not know anything about business. Rather educate them first. Hence if you see the children of multi-millionaires, they are taken to business schools, so that when the business owners die, the businesses may remain moving and not depreciating.

A foolish son will get his father's business and not manage to proceed it for a decade. A foolish daughter would inherit the business of her mother and not be able to maintain it. Only the wise in business can maintain it well, ones having business eyes, to see business in everything they look at.

The seventh rule is general, speaking about your life, emotions, reactions, decision. That "Do right, even if it is not good". In life you can do things which feel good to do them, but not being right. Things like killing a person, it can sometimes feel good, especially if it was revenge. But that is not right at all, not right to the eye of humanity. Alternatively, you can do what is right, and not feel good about it. You can invest a lot of money, well calculated, but because of trust issues, not feel good about it. That is right to do, investment is right, but might not always be good to you. You might be left tarnished after an investment.

I remember meeting one man who is old and white at Doornfontein train station, waiting for the train back in 2018. To me he looked like a homeless person, he was dirty and seemed like he does not eat right. We started speaking little, until we spoke about investments, where he told me about an investment he made, that he suddenly took all his pension money into property.

He bought land with a house inside, rejuvenated the house, so that he can start renting out the rooms there. At that time, he was living in a rented room. What he did, without argument, was right. To invest. Yet some might argue that he is renting a house while having a house, but he will be making more money from there to buy another house where he would stay in. You, see? But at that moment, it was not good to do what he did, because though he had money and property, but he looked homeless.

Yet his state would not remain forever that way, he would soon be flourishing more than thoughts can comprehend. If someone would have chosen what is good to the body, which is sparring the sacrifice that the old man did, and buy property, get in and rent out other few rooms that would not put in as much money as it did with that old man. That is how good and right separate the poor and the rich. The poor like doing the good than doing the right, spending for the happiness of their bodies, that is very good to the body, emotions, but as for the future, they will keep revolving in one place for long.

The rich do more right than good, where for some time you see them as if they are poor, but it is just a matter of time. Then when they flourish humongous, the poor would say it is witchcraft if they be black skinned, or crime, then say it is the privileges of being white if it is a white skinned person. The fact is that, not all white people are privileged; yes, there are the privileged, but some they must work down their butts to get to where they need to get to. Doing more right than good. Right for the fact that it leads them to almost maximum flourishing.

Sometimes people take decisions they think are right when not. To know if something is right, one must do serious risk and benefit calculation, then sacrifice as much as possible. Sacrificing is one of the factors separating good and right, since it is right to sacrifice to a calculated matter, but it does not feel good at that moment.

You can do something good not being right. Because good is just a feeling and thoughts, while right is an action, accomplishment of following certain principles to a prosperous land. Rule eight is taken from the seventh, but it goes further into the art of hustling. Because business needs a hustling individual, one who can pull strings to get things done, even when it does not feel good, but being right. "The spider's hunting place is where it lives, it lives in the hustle".

This is general; it can go as far as you spend nights and nights thinking on a booming strategy to let your business prosper. You must live in the hustle grounds, spend more of your time if not all, hustling, pushing hard to get things done. Even if you reach a great level no one ever reached, do not stop, stay in the hustle.

Sir Maponya lived in the hustle, he passed away having accomplished more, because when he succeeded in one thing, he did not stop, he kept on living in the hustle. A spider does not retire hunting, nor leaves its web even when it has caught enough prey, enough food. It knows it has more capabilities to get more. When you have a brand, proceed with passion to get a rank, all the way to a mall, to more than I can mention. But remember to start small while thinking big, where the procedure to move from small to big is when you live in the hustle.

You will catch big ideas, good ideas, best ideas, do not stop there, keep on living in the hustle. I am not saying retire from church, from parenting, from brothering, no, you live with those while in the hustle, in business. Whatever life you live, hustle is part of it. You are a businessman going to church, attending the matters of church and able to enable the church to reach higher heights. I know of pastors who are businessmen on the side, and able to manage a church, or even several churches fully. So, how hard will parenting be if one can do these? Being a parent to the whole congregation, what more of your family members?

You have heard many people perhaps, saying success require sacrifice, that is very true. But I come to you and say, "Success require sacrifice, but never sacrifice what is permanent". This rule, a business eye will hate it, because it is trying to decrease the evil of business to humanity, by making businessmen and businesswomen to consider humanity, their roots.

You can sacrifice temporary things like money, inheritance, but never sacrifice the life of a person. You can sacrifice a relationship. I have done that many times, sacrificing the relationships I had, because of pursuit of success, but I never sacrifice what I know I cannot bring back. Because sacrifice in business should be the sacrifice of what you can be able to return. That sounds like not a sacrifice, but it is, because you are being able to return that sacrifice, does not mean you will.

For instance, I might not bring back the relationships I have sacrificed, but I am able to do it. It is not impossible for me to bring them back, but for the sake of success, I do not want to bring them back, though I loved them. That is sacrifice. If I kill someone for success, then it would mean it is impossible to bring them back. That is evil. EVIL. Yes, the more you increase success, the greater the sacrifices you will need, but do not sacrifice what is permanent.

Sacrifice and investment sometimes cannot be separated, but they are different. With investment, it is always a sacrifice, but not all sacrifices are an investment, because they do not all assure you of a comeback. "Investment is like a sperm cell; it needs an egg cell of its kind to reproduce". The sperm cell acts as finances, the sacrifices which are in a form of investment, while the egg cell is like the idea, a ripe idea which is well suited for that kind of an investment. You need a suitable mind-set when investing, or if you try to give a chicken egg cell a person's sperm cell, without much controversy, it will be a waste. That kind of investment is lost.

You need the right thoughts, the right company's idea. Because when you invest in small businesses, you do not invest in a name, nor a friend's company, but in the idea. If you love the idea, you put it in, even if it might be your enemy, if right procedures are followed.

The twelfth says, "Business collaboration can either be a plant by the river side, or a tree by the kraal's gate", it means that when you form business friendship between different businesses, business will either loss or gain because of the other. It is very rare to find mutual benefits in a collaboration of two businesses.

One business might gain more than the other. The business is evil in its own nature, so, even to its friends it is lethal, parasitic. The tree by the river side gets water, gains more than the water. This kind of a business can be the one that is small, and it is being raised, or cared for by another big business in the society. In this case, the big business gains nothing but the fact that it has adopted a baby it has to raise.

Then the tree by the kraal's gate is a business that has collaborated with a more cunning business, where it is being used to perform certain duties, to feed the cow as it goes to feed on serious lunch, or when it comes back from serious feasts. Then it uses that small business to push small agendas. This kind of small business will not last, because it is being milked by a bigger business.

So, when investing, invest in the idea, when you collaborate, collaborate with a business where your business will benefit more, until it can grow independent and be able to collaborate with smaller businesses. If you collaborate with a business of the same size as yours, then let that business carry an idea which will progress your idea, not the one that has the same idea as yours, because it would act like an enemy, being too close, might steal few things from you and flee.

Rule thirteen "Skeletons are not in secret by mistake, keep you deep business ideas a secret". This works also in collaborations and so forth, to conceal the intentions of you own business, but show just a piece of them. Your big ideas are the hidden structures which when broken, the business will suffer. Keep them secret. Do not uncover all your business ideas, because not just that someone with more resources can use that idea quickly, but also with the fact that you are more likely to fail in that mission. Yes, you do need to tell your ideas when pitching for collaboration or sponsorship, but never tell your deep secrets. It is the nature of a person that once they speak more without action; they tend to not make it. You would like to succeed anyhow, so, conceal your deepest ideas. The ideas are the things you wish and see your business going to.

The levels you see reaching, tell the nearer ones, the nearer levels, not the final levels. To also help in being unpredictable, because it is true that people buy what they do not know sometimes, they pay for the knowledge they do not have, if you tell them everything, they might not pay for your ideas. Keep them surprised. Save your big ideas, tell the small ones, but notice that your very small ideas can be big ideas in the ears of someone. Keep it cool. Imagine if you tell an idea that is greater than the idea of the company you are pitching to, it might turn your business into a tree by the kraal's gate.

Rule fourteen "One who climbs a big tree, start with branches and small trees first". So, likewise, one who accomplish a very big idea, they start by accomplishing small ideas and duties. You start small, do small while thinking big, on your way to doing big. If you want a factory of certain products, you start with those products in the absence of the factory and see how accomplishable it is. Business in this case does not care how resourceful you are. If you start big without starting small, you might easily fall hard.

Rule fifteen "Have more conversations in your head, than in your mouth". This is a sub-rule, meant to protect rule thirteen. To protect your deep secrets, do not think aloud, think silently. Think big while speaking small. This also helps to not intimidate your potential sponsors. Because though sponsors buy the idea, but they might be intimidated and do more harm instead of good. Because they also are concealing their own deep reasons for giving away resources, so, you keep yours too. Keep those deep ideas, those deep plans. Give the small ones, which are small enough to shake mountains.

Rule sixteen; "Air is a mixture of different gases, together they are effective in shaking anything they touch, able to bring life to a suffocating specie, and able to be a need for societal activities". This rule is for those who are not as resourceful as others, to accomplish their business ideas, they need to mix with others who will be resourceful in their business. But as it has been alluded before, you will need to calculate and allow specific people in your business. If you are dealing with sales of fat cakes, and you notice that you need to sell online and you do not know how to, then collaborate with someone who will be able to. Having calculated well. One asks, how do I calculate well? It goes back to the previous talks we had, that in any move, the business should gain, and gain even in the future. Not to gain now and lose later. Like with loans, some businesses do not do proper calculations. They take loans, boom now, but when they repay the loan, they go more backward than even where they were. That is a none calculated business move.

The seventeenth rule is the whole book brought to you compendiously so, that; "Business is evil, it gains only when others loose". Why would you have to know this rule? It is this entire writing composed in one sentence. This rule is the very grandfather of all the sixteen rules. Because they exist because business is evil, and hence want to gain more than the others. All the previous rules are at the goal of ensuring business gain more at the expense of others.

Whether it be people of businesses. The previous ones are principles, and this one acts like a nature, but it is a principle too. Because you will need to master this principle for you to have more chances of accomplishing any idea you catch. I say catch because ideas are flying on the atmosphere, it takes a mind that thinks out of the box, into the atmosphere to catch those ideas. Not to make ideas out of seeing other's ideas, but that is not much of a problem.

One who avoids this nature of business, this principle, they tend to have less chances of booming in a business arena. They tend to visit the business cosmos for a moment and disappear, then later say business is not their thing. It is sometimes, but mostly so, that they feel for people more than business. In that way, they have become a charity, not a business. Business does not care you are sick or not, it wants to gain, like the grave which no matter how much you feed it, it is never full. But you must limit the food you give it, because it is evil, and when out of control, it can even consume the very owners. Do not let it be out of the plan, provided the plan is not more than evil. Because business takes what you feed it, and it will grow and become that thing you have fed it to be.

Chapter Eight

Motivations to excellence and Investments

It is quite sorrowful to me that this is my last conversation with you. But I hope by this far you have gained some more useful knowledge, and that you have caught ideas already, which you would like to execute. Having had knowledge of what to start and where to start. I hope we will have another conversation, even if not of this kind, but one where I can also listen to you. But anyway, in a business beginning, many need motivations. That is not wrong at all, but motivations are not enough.

Motivations act like fuel, they get finished as you move, and soon you will need further motivations to proceed moving. It reminds me of students who lack the inner push to study, but they would watch endless videos on internet to be kept motivated. So that they can move further with studies. This kind of need for success, where a person needs to be motivated is not a good one, but still right. It is best if someone has an inner force first, then motivations act like paraffin to an already burning flame. Just like a truck with fuel, but needs a push to start, motivations are like that to some. They act as kick-starts.

To give a passionate person immediate fires to start moving, but like fire made with papers, motivations get ineffective as time elapses. Hence a greater thing than motivations is needed.

There are people who do not need motivation at all; they are well furnished inside-out. They got the passion, the desire, resources, and right knowledge to start moving on their own. These people do exist but are as rare as finding a red bird in the middle of Johannesburg city. Not easy, nor impossible. So, if you feel like you need motivation, take it. Sometimes we have almost everything, but lack resources, motivation come to show you that you can use what you must get what you want. Though some people depend totally on motivations, and their work is less, because fires made by papers do not last, they at least do something. They would dream to buy a car but end up buying a bicycle. Is that not success? But small, isn't it? That is the effect of only motivational push to any business.

If a business is pushed by motivations, it starts off, but never reach far. It will need constant motivations to keep moving. It depends on the motivations for it to exist. Thus, I come to you to advice that you shouldn't depend on the motivations to move, let them just give you that little push, and then passion and love drive you forward to the dream land. That is what motivations are good for.

You might be wondering, what exactly the motivations are. Well, they are anything you read, hear, taste, touch from the outward world, which stirs up the inside with so much great force that you will start to do something. If you listen to a motivator, you will be moved. But once the motion starts for a minute, and you no longer hear that motivator, you end up stopping.

What if you keep receiving that motivation? You will go on with the movement, until that motivation is no longer able to move you. Also, look at how constantly body builders watch motivational videos, wearing motivating items. They fill their surrounding with motivations, to constantly create those paper fires, and they keep moving. Some see not much success, and they drop out, some proceed, because some have passion to be fit.

One of the problems with motivations is that they only give you the feeling that your muscles are enough to make a change, but never give you the actual muscles. Motivations tend to make you appreciate what you have, and how you can get what you need and want to get, but never get it for you. Also, they do not make you too strong against challenges.

Usually when challenges come, motivations weaken. Because people start to notice that motivations are factual, while challenges are realistic. These motivations become evil when they define who you are, and you believe it. When they find you not knowing yourself, and they give you a definition of who you are. Allowing the thoughts of someone to define you. Look at yourself, define yourself. Not because of situations but look who you have remained to be in all situations, not who you are in one situation. Because situations change, personalities change, but the actual person doesn't change.

What motivations can be good at is to complete the incomplete desires, incomplete passions for business or anything in life. They are for reaching excellence, but on their own, it is not easy to drive one from where they are, without passion, to total excellence. I hope you do notice that some people have passion, but need a little motivation to start moving, because they sometimes ignore the passion to do new things, because they have not seen anything new done by someone close-by, or they do not think they can do something new. Of not just adapting to change but implementing the change. That is where motivations are good, to reveal the flame, to increase the flames.

As for investments, that is what every business need. Investments are like milk they are a need to every baby. The type of investment done does determine the type of the next action that can be taken. For instance, if you make a small investment towards buying a car, surely you will not be buying a big car, but a second hand. Unless you get loans. Investments need patience, and proper planning.

Someone should not invest without planning, because they will be someone getting breast milk when there is no baby to drink. You need a good business plan, then a good time manageable plan for the finances invested. You cannot plan to save 5 million bucks for a 5 million bucks costing asset over a period of five years without including inflation to your planning. You will save those 5 million bucks, then five years later, the item you needed is double the initial price. Let any savings or investments be timely, time flexible and time manageable.

Savings and investments differ, a lot. Savings are a little risky than investments, and they are less beneficial than investments. Savings are just the coat of the water surface, where you can only get back the dead fish you put there. It is floating, so just as you put it, you find it as it is. But investments are the depths of the waters. It is when you use one fish to get more fish, or one worm to get plenty fish. But you plan and predict the results before you even start the action. With investments, you are not certain that what you put in will yield what you expect. Sometimes you go fishing with 15 worms, and return with two fish, or none. But sometimes you go fishing with only two worms and return with enough fish to fill a taxi. It only depends on the planning, the place you will get that fish from and the knowledge of how fish live and behave together with the action relative to the planning.

Someone might find a good spot of fishing but end up getting only three fish due to the little materials they have. If you invest 5 bucks for few months, you cannot expect to get over 5 thousand bucks in return. You must sacrifice more, for you to get more. It is a principle. And never rush to get quick bucks because you should not forget that business is evil. There can be no loss in business and gain of the people more than what the business gain. What I mean is, you cannot just spend airtime and receive a lot of cash, or just spend few bucks and instantly get a lot of money in return. That is not investment, rather is gambling. Because though someone might have gotten that instant money, it does not mean you will get it. And the fact that you got that instant money, it does not mean someone else will get it. Unless it is charity, not a business.

It is advertising, to draw more people nearby. Like those big palaces of gambling, a person can win over 500 000 bucks in a single day, that means they gain more than that from the individuals who try to get that much 500 000. The gambling business manage and program the machines to allow only limited people to win, lucky are they, but the rest will lose dismally so. Imagine if no one won, will people try it?

No, so the winnings are used to call people, are like the worms used to draw more fish nearer. And when people come, they are snatched. If a gambling business was losing more than it gains, then it was not going to hire stuff, cleaners, and so forth. But because it gains even more thousand times than the loses it makes, and then it can even sponsor students to study at varsity.

So, never let your investment be in gambling, because it is not investment at all, but gambling, highest risk, like trying to fish a shark, you can, but you also put yourself in great danger. Well, some investments are like a net, you only use materials around you to get fish. When I speak about fish here, I vividly speak of gains, profit. Using the net, you do not need the great sacrifice like a worm, all you need is to use the resources you have in a proper place, and you will gain. It is like someone who wants to buy a car to transport students around. Instead of investing money in the bank, or in other assets, they do not risk the money, but rather start selling fat cakes and so forth, using the very little they have, increasingly so, with the goal to buy a car. It seems impossible yes, but it is not. Only that we rarely see it, but it happens. I know of a man who got a truck from his father, sold it, and bought materials for making party stages and so forth. As I speak, he has over four cars now, in just less than 5 years. He did not risk money, but used what he had, resources.

I hope by now you see something about motivations and investments. On how they can be rightly utilized to move. Just to comment a little bit more on them before I go cook. I am a good cook, but sadly I have specific menu, and recipe. Anyway, motivations can push you to take the last penny you have to investments without calculations. You are risking even the risk itself. You need to plan, no matter how great the flames induced by the motivations are.

But sadly, sometimes exactly after planning, the desires end, the fires cool off and you no longer move, because the further motivations to proceed the fires are not there. You cannot listen to the same video of motivation every day and be effectively motivated to make great motions, you will need deeper motivations, greater motivations. And if not there, then there is no more motion.

I know of people who are partially motivated by someone's biography to start a business, then when they get home, there is no fire, no force to start even the very planning. Some receive serious fires to start planning but fail to proceed to work. Some receive excess fires to get home, plan and even act, but if there is no passion, the business will fall in times of trials. It would be like laying a foundation on sand, when soil erosion and other challenges come, the house shakes and loses life. It collapses.

My friend, if you have no passion for a specific business, then do not feel the little fires of motivation and start a business. Rather know what you have passion in, then take those little fires the motivations have created, invest them in that passionate business you have. When you take the fires into a business you are not passionate about, then you will only receive failure, and at least you learn from failure, but instead you could have converted that failure into great success. Because motivations plus passion, with rightfully calculated investments, you are destined to great success.

It is good to know a way to succeed instead of looking for failure. We do learn through failure but let us try by all the weapons we have, to succeed, not fail. When failure come, let it come, finding you having used what you have for success, and use that failure to learn to perfect the piece of planning next time. Because sometimes we fail from the planning we made, a good plan but not right for business. Sometimes our plans are good, but our actions are not proportional to plans, hence we get to fail. Like someone having a study timetable, but not follow it, they might fail, isn't it?

Then there are those who plan right, and act according to the plan, but fail. That is rare, but it happens. In this one, there are factors attached to it. Factors like the company they move with, the time they are using that plan in. You can plan rightly, but in a wrong interval of time. The plan must include right timing.

I seem to have said enough thus far. Though I still wish to proceed with the conversation, but I must pause here. Hopefully, we shall meet again in another set of conversations, discussing further topics. Amid all I said, all I was trying to put to the table is already there. That business is evil. And we should know that and not prevent it from being evil, but only prevent it from being more than evil. I have spoken about all that affect a business and how a business behave, and in all that I hope you have been equipped with rightful weapons of knowledge to plan, use right materials, do right rather than just good, sacrifice in good calculations and act rightly so.

I haven't spoken about how you can rightfully calculate an investment. But I must cease the talk here, until we can have another chance to meet and speak about something else, in which I might include the ways to rightfully calculate investments.

Business does not have race, nor any gender. So, anyone can do business, every tribe, every language, every village, every town, city, and group of people have a business. Do not let the opportunity of making that business idea boom to go to waste, by not acting on it. Learn to have free time where you just sit and think. There is power in thinking. If you have not caught that business idea, sit down sometimes, just alone, in a quite area. Allow the mind to be free and not disturbed. They call it meditation, but I cannot say that, since you might think there are restrictions and rules set for what I am advising.

Rather, just think, do not think too much, but think deep. You will catch that idea which when you caught, it would shake mountains and even make your blood start flowing at a different rate. Believe in it, plan on it, invest, sacrifice. Do as much as you can, day and night to implement that idea. And do not have only one business idea. Have several, in several fields. But be patient to allow each idea to mature in action.

Having several ideas help one to stand even during natural disasters. I recall the ladies who sold at school, they might have had only that idea of selling at school. Then when the Corona Virus Infectious Disease 2019 (Covid-19) stroke, they were no longer able to sell at schools. So, they needed an alternative, which is selling at the streets. They are to receive new experience and challenges. Whereas they could have thought of going to the streets after selling at school, they would have gained enough experience to sell at the streets, and not worry when the pandemic came along.

It is like having a single baby, it is very easy for you to be childless since challenges strike day and night. So, give birth to few children, when one dies, you still have others to keep. Think wide, always think, not too much, but deep enough to catch big ideas. If you are afraid of thinking, you will only act on what others thought, and be a slave to their implemented thoughts. Whereas you can think and act according to what you think. Until we meet again hopefully in another conversation, keep thinking and implementing those ideas friend. That when we meet, we might update each other of great success we have individually made.

Mini Lexicon: Induce- to start, to begin something anew.
Philo- to love, it is a word from Greek, meaning passion.